THAT

BIT
to
ROWN

THIS RABBIT IS
NOT FOR SALE.
AND HIS
NAME IS NOT
BUNNYWUNNY
ITS STANLEY
— Emily Brown

FOR
LITTLE DOG,
BOWY, BEARY
AND CAT
— FOR MANY YEARS OF
FAITHFUL SERVICE — C.C.

FOR
RUPERT,
JOHN MILK,
ELE AND THE
BIZZ — N.L.

HODDER CHILDREN'S BOOKS

First published in 2006

This edition published in 2016   2

Text © Cressida Cowell 2006   Illustrations © Neal Layton 2006

The moral rights of the author and illustrator have been asserted.

All rights reserved.

A CIP catalogue record for this book is available from the British Library.

ISBN 978 1 444 92341 4

Printed in China

Hodder Children's Books

An imprint of Hachette Children's Group

Part of Hodder and Stoughton

Carmelite House

50 Victoria Embankment

London EC4Y 0DZ

An Hachette UK Company

www.hachette.co.uk

www.hachettechildrens.co.uk

Insides designed by David Mackintosh,

cover designed by Jennifer Stephenson.

MIX
Paper from
responsible sources
FSC® C104740
www.fsc.org

THAT RABBIT belongs to EMILY BROWN

written by
CRESSIDA COWELL
illustrated by
NEAL LAYTON

Hodder
Children's
Books

Once upon a time,
there was a little girl called Emily Brown
and an old grey rabbit called Stanley.

One day, Emily Brown and Stanley were just launching themselves into Outer Space to look for alien life forms, when there was a **Rat-a-tat-tat!** at the kitchen door.

It was the Chief Footman to the Queen.
He said,

Emily Brown looked at the Queen's teddy bear.
It was stiff and new and gold and *horrible*.
It had staring eyes and no smile at all.

"No thank you," said Emily Brown. "This rabbit is NOT for sale.
And his name isn't Bunnywunny. It's STANLEY."

And Emily Brown shut the door politely.

An hour or so later, Emily Brown and Stanley were just riding through the Sahara Desert on their motorbike, when there was a **Rat-a-tat-tat!** at the garden door.

It was the Army.
The Captain saluted and said,

"Her Most Royal Highness Queen Gloriana the Third greets Miss Emily Brown, and she would still like to have that Bunnywunny. In return, she offers her the brand-new golden teddy bear, and ten talking dolls that say 'Mama Mama'."

Emily Brown said, "I don't want ten talking dolls.
I want my rabbit. And his name isn't Bunnywunny.
It's STANLEY."

And Emily Brown sent that Army away, less politely this time.

A few days later, Emily Brown and Stanley
were just deep-sea diving off the Barrier Reef,
when there was a **Rat-a-tat-tat!** at the garden door.

It was the Navy.
The Admiral saluted and said,

"MAMA!"

"Her Most Glorious Royalness Queen Gloriana the Third, greets Miss Emily Brown, and she would like you to hand over that rabbit at your earliest convenience. She points out that she is the poshest person on the planet, and Bunnywunny will be much better off with HER. In return, she offers you the brand-new golden teddy bear, ten talking dolls that say *Mama Mama*, and fifty rocking horses that rock for ever."

"I don't care WHO she is," said Emily Brown.
"This rabbit belongs to ME.
And his name isn't Bunnywunny. It's STANLEY."

And she sent that Navy away.

A few weeks later, Emily Brown and Stanley were just climbing through the Amazonian rainforest, when there was a **Rat-a-tat-tat!** on the garden door.

It was the Air Force.
The Wing Commander saluted
and said,

"Her Excellence the Most Mighty Queen Gloriana the Third, greets Miss Emily Brown, and says she must have the Bunnywunny RIGHT NOW or SHE WILL NOT ANSWER FOR THE CONSEQUENCES.

In return, we will give her a brand-new golden teddy bear, ten talking dolls that say 'Mama Mama'...

Now Emily Brown was FED UP!

She sent that Air Force away and she pinned a big notice
on the garden gate that read:

A few months later, Emily Brown and Stanley were lying fast asleep in bed, dreaming of all the adventures they would have the next day, when there was absolutely no noise at all at the door, or the gate, or the window.

Shhh!!

Silently, in crept the Queen's Special Commandos...

and they STOLE the rabbit that belonged to Emily Brown.

When Emily Brown woke up the next morning,
for the first time in her life there was

NO STANLEY!

Emily Brown was SO CROSS.
She knew just what had happened.
She marched straight up to the Palace on the Hill.

She knocked on that naughty Queen's front door.

Rat-a-tat-tat!

Emily Brown ran into the Palace
and there was that naughty Queen, crying like
anything. The first thing she said was,

"Thank goodness you've come, Emily Brown. There's something wrong with Bunnywunny!"

There was indeed something wrong with Stanley.
That silly naughty Queen had put him in the Royal Washing Machine
all night and he'd come out an odd pink colour.

The Royal Dressmakers had stuffed him full of stuffing so he wasn't flippy-floppy any more. And, worst of all, they had sewn up his mouth, where Emily Brown had picked it away, and Stanley wasn't smiling any more.

Stanley was MISERABLE.

"Oh, Emily Brown, *Emily Brown*, is there anything you can do?" asked the silly naughty Queen.

"There certainly is," said Emily Brown,

"I shall take Stanley HOME."

That silly Queen started crying harder than ever. "I have all the toys in the world but none as nice as STANLEY."

Queen Gloriana the Third

Emily Brown felt sorry for that silly Queen,
so she went to the Royal Toy Cupboard and she
took down that brand-new golden teddy bear and
she placed it on the Queen's lap.

MAMA!

Emily Brown whispered so that
no one else could hear,

"You take that horrid brand-new
teddy bear and you **play with him
all day. Sleep with him at night.
Hold him very tight and be
sure to have lots of adventures.**
And then maybe one day you
will wake up with a real toy
of your OWN."

And Emily Brown and Stanley went home.

That was the last Emily Brown and Stanley heard from
that silly naughty Queen for quite some time.

But one day, a couple of years later, just as Emily Brown and Stanley were exploring the Outermost Regions of the Milky Way...

there came a **Rat-a-tat-tat!** on the kitchen door...

It was the Postman with a letter for Emily Brown.

And it just said:

Queen Gloriana the Third

Thank you.